Zack and his Gramps liked to go down to the model boating lake, which was close to Gramps's house. In the summer, there were regattas on the lake. Lots of big model sailing boats took part in them. Zack had a little model boat, but it was too small to compete with the big ones.

Zack and Gramps wished they had a big sailing boat too. Gramps sent off for a kit as he was very good at building things.

When it arrived, Zack helped Gramps make a model sailing boat from the kit. It took them a long time.

The boat was made of plastic. She had tall sails with ribbon flags at the top and an extra set of sails for windy weather. They called her "Jacamar." Gramps made a stand for the boat's long keel, and they sat her on a shelf in his living room.

When she was completely finished, Gramps and Zack took Jacamar to the boating lake. They set her on the lake and off she sailed.

"She looks fantastic!" said Zack.
"Yes," Gramps agreed.

Zack ran around the lake and was just in time to stop Jacamar from crashing into the side. Then he sailed her back to Gramps. It was windy and there were quite big waves on the lake.

Jacamar bobbed up and down.

Zack and Gramps sailed Jacamar back and forth across the lake. Suddenly, they spotted that she was starting to sink.

"Come on!" Zack begged the boat. "Sail a bit more. You can do it!" He stretched his arm out and tried his hardest to get hold of her.

But it was no good. Jacamar was just too far out on the lake.

"Help! She is sinking!" shouted Zack, starting to panic. Soon only the boat's flags were left sticking out of the lake. "Gramps!" he wailed miserably.

Gramps ran around the side of the boating lake to Zack. Without stopping to worry about his boots or trousers, he stepped into the lake and started to wade out.

It got deeper and deeper but Gramps kept going. As soon as he got to where the boat's flags were sticking up, he grabbed them.

He lifted up the boat and waved at Zack, who clapped and jumped about on the side of the lake. Gramps staggered back to give Zack the Jacamar.

Zack took the boat and then helped Gramps out of the lake. Gramps was very wet and muddy.

"Thank you! I'm so glad you saved her!" cried Zack, giving Gramps a big hug.

Gramps gave Zack a wet smile.

"I think we had better go home," he said.

At home, Zack helped as Gramps dried himself off. Then they examined Jacamar together.

"She must have a hole in her somewhere," Gramps explained. They looked and looked for it until Gramps spotted a small metal pipe sticking out of the hull. "There!" he exclaimed. "We must have forgotten to fill that when we made her."

Gramps filled in the end of the little metal pipe.

"There we are, all finished!" he said, and smiled at Zack. "When that has dried, we can take her to the lake. She will not sink this time."

Next weekend, Zack and Gramps went down to the boating lake again with Zack proudly carrying Jacamar.

There were lots of boats sailing on the lake, as there was going to be a regatta. Zack and Gramps hoped to take part this time.

Zack entered Jacamar in the regatta for children under ten. He set the sails and waited for the start.

CRACK! went the starter's pistol, and Zack let go of Jacamar.

She skimmed across the lake with the rest of the boats.

"Come on, come on, Jacamar!" Zack shouted, loudly.

He ran around to the far side of the lake to catch his boat. Then back across the lake she sailed.

"Come on, come on!" shouted Gramps. "You can do it! Come on, Zack!"

“Well,” said Zack, at the end of the regatta. “We did not win, but I had a brilliant time. Can we bring Jacamar to the next regatta, too, Gramps?”

“Yes,” smiled Gramps, “and perhaps next time we will win.”

Zack and Gramps went home together, with Zack still proudly carrying Jacamar.